Rathbone the Rat

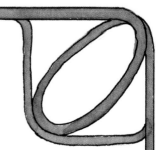

Patricia Derrick
Shirley O'Neil

Rathbone the Rat

Illustrated by
J-P Loppo Martinez

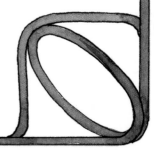

He's Rathbone the Rat,
In his bri-ght red hat.
A hustling, bustling,
Scurrying Rat.

With a scowl on his face,
That matches his frown.
He hides in the subway
That circles our town.

He travels down the alleys
And long narrow streets.
Looking for delicious,
Delectable sweets.

Then he says to himself
With a sigh of relief,
"I think I just found
My midnight treat!"

Rathbone the Rat, a mis-chie-vi-ous Rat
Rathbone the Rat, a mis-chie-vi-ous Rat

He hides in the corners of grocery store owners.
Dines on the fine cheeses as much as he pleases.

Rathbone decided
The food sounded great.
Like the food he just ate
On the store's **silver plates!**

Rathbone the Rat, a mis-chie-vi-ous Rat
Rathbone the Rat, a mis-chie-vi-ous Rat

An announcement came at dinner.
The store owners delivered the plates.
But the silver plates were bare.
No food was found, anywhere!

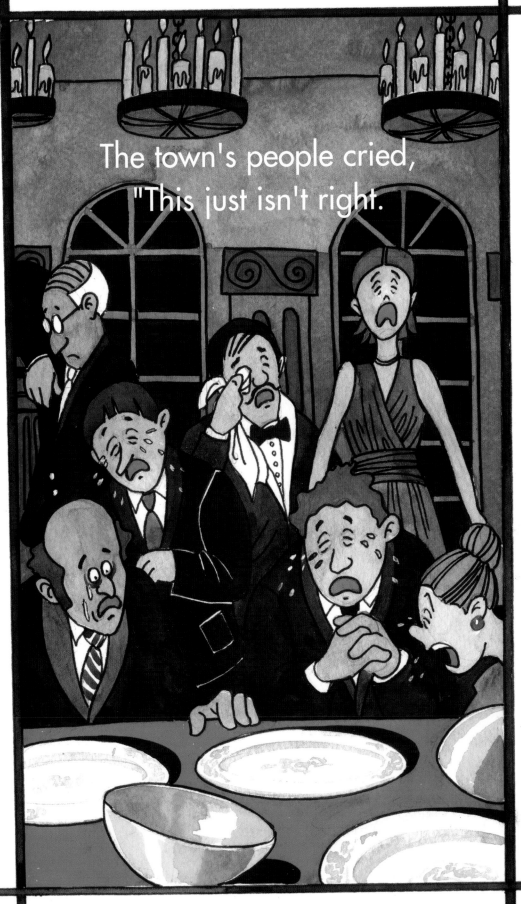

The town's people cried,
"This just isn't right.

Who ate all of our food on this special night?"

Catalina the Cat looked at Rathbone.
He's been her long time friend.
But Catalina knew it was him,
And said, "When will this nonsense end?"

Rathbone the Rat, a mis-chie-vi-ous Rat
Rathbone the Rat, a mis-chie-vi-ous Rat

Rathbone was sad and felt very bad.
He wanted to make amends.

Then Rathbone took charge
As they went through the town.
And Friends were helping
From all around.

They brought plenty of food
And filled all the silver plates
Everyone was happy
So they sat down and ate.

Catalina the Cat
Could once again see,
What a kindly Rat,
Rathbone could be.

But with a grin on his face,
He scurried away.
If you listened closely,
You could hear him say,

"A new adventure,
I'm off to find.
But what I've learned,
I'll *try to keep in mind.*"

Rathbone the Rat, a mis-chie-vi-ous Rat
Rathbone the Rat, a mis-chie-vi-ous Rat

Rathbone the Rat

Lyrics Patricia Derrick - Music J-P Loppo Martinez

Three R's Before Reading

Rhythm • Rhyme • Repetition

Three R's before Reading (Rhythm, Rhyme and Repetition) uses multi-sensory stimulation to fire neurons in the brain. Multi-sensory stimulation creates strong connections between neurons. With strong connections, learning becomes easier.

Rhythm is found in music and movement. Rhythm is experienced when we listen to musical sounds, decipher what is heard and move to the beat. Children will literally get up on their feet and start dancing when they hear "foot tapping" music. Children will want to participate when they hear rhythm. Participation can include everything that makes up a "multi-sensory" experience for the child.

Rhyme: Rhyming verses provide patterns. Patterns are found in poetry, rhyming books and in musical songs. Children love the sound of patterns. They can feel what they hear throughout their bodies. Patterns stimulate the right side of the brain. The right side of the brain is responsible for math and spatial relationships, as well as language.

Repetition: Children love to repeat stimulating experiences over and over again. When children ask to do an activity again, they are really saying, "I want to feel those sensations again." Children feel sensations when the activity is "multi-sensory". If a child is given an opportunity to participate in a multi-sensory book, the child will want to read that particular book over and over again.

Animalations books provide multi-sensory stimulation and make learning easier for children.

Teacher Parent Activities

Rathbone the Rat and other Animalations books provide opportunities for learning experiences beyond reading a book. Adapt the suggested activities to provide age appropriate learning for all children participating in Rathbone the Rat.

Movement:
Give children an opportunity to express themselves through movement as they listen to Rathbone the Rat. Role play how a rat might dance to the music.

Social:
Discuss where Rathbone the Rat lives: Paris France. Find Paris on a world globe and talk about how far away it is. Talk about how Rathbone dines on fine cheeses and then brags to his friends. Is Rathbone taking advantage of others? Would you do something like that to a friend?

Discuss how Rathbone feels remorse and tries to make amends with the help of his friend, Catalina the Cat. What does Rathbone do at the end of the book?

Talk about how we treat others and what we can do to be good members of our community. Give the children opportunities to act out various character parts in the book. How does it feel to be Rathbone? How does it feel to be Catalina the Cat? Do you have a friend like Catalina the Cat?

Music:
Encourage the children to participate in the music by singing. Give children opportunities to be Rathbone the Rat as they sing the song.

Art:
Make a drawing of the town dinner and all the silver plates. Possibly make more than one drawing with the silver plates bare and with the silver plates filled with food.

Language:
Provide opportunities for children to explain their drawings to others in the group. Self esteem will "sizzle" as children share their work with others. Invite children to read their work to family members, friends, and grandparents, as well as post their drawings on home refrigerators to share with others over and over.

A rat is a small rodent. Mice and squirrels are also rodents. Rats are usually considered pests, although some people keep rats as pets in their homes. Rats usually travel at night and are active.

Rats build nests under buildings, low shrubs or ground cover, wood piles, and garbage dumps. They can also be found in walls, attics, vines or trees.

Rats kept as pets are usually purchased in a pet store. Owners of rats consider rats to be fine pets. Pet rats are known for their intelligence, playfulness and sociability. They are extremely clean. Rats can be taught tricks, and entertain their owners in the same way other domesticated animals entertain their owners.

This book is dedicated to the animals in our zoos
and zoo keepers who keep them healthy and content.
On behalf of all young visitors, thank you for the
delightful and educational experience.

Patricia Derrick, Author

Master of Education from the University of Utah
Early Childhood and Elementary School Educator
Owner and Operator of Early Learning Schools: 30 years
Assistant Professor, Metropolitan State College, Mesa College Campus, GJ Colorado

Author Patricia Derrick is available for speaking engagements and conferences
Email: info@animalations.com for more information

Mr. Walrus and the Old School Bus

Publishing
4186 Melodia Songo Court
Las Vegas, Nevada 89135

ISBN # 1-933818-17-4
ISBN # 978-1-933818-17-7

Complimentary replacement CD's for libraries:
Send requests to: info@animalations.com

Printed in Korea

Also Available from Animalations:

Farley the Ferret of Farkleberry Farm:
Farley and the farmer take bread and jam to the fair, but when the drought hit Foley County, there was no jam to share. Children danced around the vines and made silent wishes in their minds. Find out what happened to the berries on Farkleberry Farm. Message: Farley and the children found a way to help others.

Riley the Rhinoceros:
Riley is called the jungle bus because he gives rides to baby animals as they find their way back home. But, he can't give rides to all the animals because that would be preposterous.
Message: ...helping others and friendship.

Rickity & Snickity at the Balloon Fiesta:
Two Rocky Mountain cubs hide in the back of the Park Rangers van to attend the Balloon Fiesta. The cubs rode in the hot air balloon with such ease, everyone thought they were celebrities. Join the fun at the Balloon Fiesta. Message: Baby animals grow to their full size very rapidly. Try to imagine bear cubs riding in a hot air balloon.

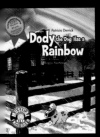

Dody the Dog has a Rainbow:
Dody the dog is lost and travels through the town and countryside looking for his home. Dody eventually finds his rainbow to help him find his way.
Message: There is hope inside your rainbow.

Sly the Dragonfly:
Sly the Dragonfly loves to fly high. "I hear the wind whistling through my wings. It makes my heart wake up and sing". Sly encourages young readers to be the best that they can be.
Message: Life is all about the way you live each day.

Montgomery the Moose:
With five distinct musical styles, Montgomery the Moose shakes his caboose for his friends. Young readers will learn to appreciate different kinds of music and participate in movement activities.
Message: If you practice enough, you can accomplish most things you would like to do.